The Wonderful World of Disney

Walt Disney
BAMBI

DERRYDALE BOOKS
New York

Twin Books

The animals in the forest woke up to the sound of birds chirping one morning. Squirrels scurried down their trees and Thumper the rabbit thumped a hollow log as hard as he could.

"Wake up! Spring has come!" he happily called. "A young prince has been born! Everyone come and see!"

Even Friend Owl, who disliked being awakened, was happy.

At Thumper's call, the animals came running to see the newborn fawn. Friend Owl flew in and nudged his way to the first row, which was also occupied by Mother Rabbit and her babies, Mrs Skunk, and Mr Raccoon.

"Oh! Isn't he lovely?" they each cried out in turn. A murmur of approval rippled through the small crowd.

"What's his name?" asked Thumper, who was a very bold bunny.

"His name is Bambi. He's very sleepy," said the doe quietly. The little fawn lay sound asleep against her.

"When will he be able to play?" asked Thumper, who wanted to show Bambi the forest and become his friend.

"In a little while, perhaps, when he wakes up," said Bambi's mother gently.

Soon Bambi opened his eyes. Then,
with a push, he stood up on his legs.
"Look! He can stand!" cried Thumper,
but the little fawn slipped to the ground
because his legs were still very wobbly.

When Bambi got back up on his feet, a strange creature startled him.

"Don't be afraid. It's a BIRD! Birds fly, and they sing, and they also build their nests in the branches of trees," explained Thumper.

"B-b-bird! BIRD!" repeated Bambi.

"Yeah, bird!" said Thumper, chuckling.

"Bird!" cried Bambi to a beautiful butterfly that flew by.

"No, that's not a bird!" laughed Thumper. "It's a BUTTERFLY!"

"B-butterfly?" echoed Bambi, a little puzzled. "Are those b-butterflies, too?" he asked, pointing at a patch of bright blossoms.

"No, those are FLOWERS," replied Thumper.

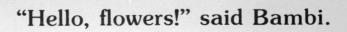

"Hello, flowers!" said Bambi.

Just then, the black-and-white tail of a young skunk popped out from the flowers.

"Flower!" said Bambi. He was very puzzled when the skunk appeared.

"You can call me Flower if you like," the skunk said shyly. "It's such a pretty name!"

He was very flattered that Bambi would mistake him for a flower.

Spring soon gave way to summer and summer to fall. The months went by and Bambi learned many things with his friend Thumper. He grew bigger and stronger, and loved to play all day long. When the autumn leaves started to fall, Bambi and Thumper spent many hours frolicking in the colorful leaves. At night, Bambi slept cuddled against his mother.

One night snowflakes gently fell from the sky.

When Bambi woke up the next morning, everything was white. He stood up, and something wet and cold fell on his head.

"Mother, what has happened?
Everything looks so different!" he cried.
"Winter is here, my darling, and the
forest will go to sleep under the snow
until the spring," she explained.
"I must go tell Thumper," said Bambi,
and he went looking for his friend.

Bambi found Thumper
sliding on the pond.

"C'mon, Bambi, let's skate!" proposed
Thumper. "It's lots of fun!"

But winters are not all fun and laughter. Bambi and his mother had to go far to find grass to eat because of the snow. One day, while they were eating, two loud gunshots tore through the forest.

"The hunters have found us! Run, Bambi!" ordered his mother.

Bambi ran fast and far, but when he turned around...

...his mother was gone. The hunters had caught her. Now Bambi was alone.

Spring followed winter at last. Owl was again awakened in the daylight, and he was not pleased.

"What kind of fool would dare shake my tree at this hour of the day?" Owl scowled. But when he looked down, he smiled. "Bambi! It's you! You've grown so much! And how handsome you look! What's that on your head?"

"These are my antlers," proudly replied Bambi. "It took me a long time to become big and strong, but my father, the Great Prince of the Forest, helped me."

"He must be very proud of you," said Friend Owl.

23

Bambi said goodbye to the owl and went off to look for Thumper. Suddenly a voice startled him.

"Hello," it said softly.

Bambi turned around. A very pretty doe peered out at him from behind a tree.

"I'm Faline," she said. "May I be your friend?"

"Why do you want to be my friend?" asked Bambi, puzzled.

"Because I like you," said Faline, blushing. And she gave Bambi a lick on the neck. Bambi blushed.

Thumper had found a
new friend as well.

"This must be what happens in the spring!" Thumper
laughed. "Everybody falls in love!"
Bambi was a little shy at first, not quite sure how to behave.
Then he decided that he liked Faline. They made a perfect pair.

Flower had also found a new friend—a pretty little girl skunk.

But another young stag named Ronno wanted Faline, too.

"She's mine!" he thundered and then charged at Bambi.

But Bambi refused to give up Faline. He charged the other young stag with all his might. With a powerful thrust, he pushed Ronno off the hill.

Faline stood by, blushing with pride.
"Are you glad I chased Ronno away?"
asked Bambi when he returned.
"Of course I am!" she said.

The next day, Bambi went up to the mountain to tell his father about Faline. "I am very happy for you, my son," said the Prince. "But beware of the hunters. They took your mother and they will come back. Take good care of Faline."

Then the great stag pointed to a plume
of smoke rising from the valley below.
"That's the hunters' campfire. You'd
better get Faline to safety now," he said.

Bambi galloped down the mountain to Faline. As he came closer, he heard dogs barking. His heart started to pound. Faline was trapped on a ledge with a pack of furious dogs snarling below her. Bambi at once charged at the pack.

As he pushed the dogs back, Faline sprang away. Bambi leaped after her.

But a shot was fired and
Bambi fell to the ground.
The bullet had wounded
him. He tried to get up,
but he was very weak.

At the hunters' camp, the campfire had
not been put out properly. The wind blew
the small flame onto some grass. Soon
roaring flames were advancing through
the forest. The dogs ran away and the
hunters did too, abandoning the hunt.

The animals ran away as well, while
the fire pursued them through the forest.

The Great Prince of the
Forest braved the fire
looking for his son.

"Bambi, what has
happened to you?" he said
when he found him.

"I've been wounded,
Father."

"You must be strong
now, my son. Get up!
Follow me! I'll take you to
a place that is safe from
the fire," he said.

Bambi followed his father through the woods. His side hurt, but he showed no pain. He thought only of Faline.

Bambi's father led him to the river bank. All the animals had taken refuge on an island in the middle of the river.

"The fire cannot cross the water," explained the great stag. "Everyone will be safe on the island."

The old prince jumped into the current and Bambi followed him. They swam to the island with powerful strokes. Faline was waiting for them on the shore. Bambi ran up to her.

"I'm so happy to see you! Are you all right?" she asked him.

"I'll be fine," said Bambi, "now that I've found you."

Soon it was spring again, and once
more Owl was awakened. "What's all
that racket?" he grumbled when he heard
Thumper thumping away.

"It's spring again, Friend Owl!" Thumper called. "I have good news: Bambi is a father!"

"Bambi is a father!" echoed the owl in disbelief. "My, my, my, time has gone by!"

Faline had given birth to twin fawns just that morning. All the forest animals came running to see the new arrivals. They could not believe their eyes.

"Look how handsome they are!" cried Thumper.

"They do look sweet, don't they?" added Flower.

"Congratulations, Faline! Congratulations, Bambi!" cheered the animals. Thumper looked around for Bambi, but he was not there.

Bambi had gone with his father up the mountain.
"I'm growing old, my son," the Great Prince said. "You must take over for me. I have taught you all I know, and it's your turn to look after the animals in the forest. Warn them of danger and of the approach of the hunters. I know you will do well."

"Thank you, Father," said Bambi. "I'll make you proud of me."

He watched his father leave. Then Bambi proudly raised his head. He was now the Great Prince of the Forest.

This 1988 edition published by Derrydale Books, distributed by Crown Publishers, Inc., 225 Park Avenue South New York, New York 10003

Produced by Twin Books
15 Sherwood Place
Greenwich, CT 06830

Directed by HELENA Productions Ltd

Image adaption by Van Gool-Lefevre-Loiseaux

Printed and bound in Hong Kong

ISBN 0-517-66193-4

hgfedcba

The Wonderful World of Disney